VU JA DE

VU JA DE

Collected Short Stories

Volume Three

by BP Gregory

Copyright © 2020 BP Gregory

All Rights Reserved

Babes Down Boreholes Copyright © 2020

Abstract Copyright © 2016

Parallel Copyright © 2020

White Picket Copyright © 2017

Our Lady of the Trampled Beast Copyright © 2019

ALL RIGHTS RESERVED. This work is copyright apart from any use permitted under the Copyright Act 1968. This work may not be reproduced or transmitted in part or in its entirety in any form or by any means, electronic or mechanical, including photocopying, recording, or by any information storage and retrieval system, nor may any other exclusive right be exercised, without the prior written consent of the author Bronwyn Purdy Gregory, except where permitted by law.

This is a work of fiction. Places and place names are either fictional, or used fictitiously. Any resemblance to persons either living or dead is purely co-incidental.

ISBN 978 0 6457319 4 1

Acknowledgments

Vu Ja De cover image by Mikbiz; Babes Down Boreholes cover image by Fernando Cortes; Abstract cover image by Pete Sherrard; Parallel cover image by Thananchai Jaipa; White Picket cover image by Gui Jun Peng; Our Lady of the Trampled Beast cover image by nito; Flora & Jim cover image by Marcel Jancovic; Orotund cover image by Alex Malikov; and Visit the House image by Peter Dedeurwaerder, all courtesy of Shutterstock. Wendigo images by BP Gregory.

Two of these stories; Babes Down Boreholes, and Our Lady of the Trampled Beast; owe great thanks to Bo Chappell. Babes Down Boreholes was originally conceived for an anthology that never got off the ground, due to extremely valid 2020 pandemic reasons. And Bo put me on to the idea of writing a wendigo-type story with Our Lady of the Trampled Beast. His kind and tireless encouragement to me and to authors from all walks of life is invaluable.

Parallel first appeared on 11th May 2020 on the excellent Kendall Reviews site, as part of their series Isolation Tales: interesting stories to help people through difficult times (a.k.a. the 2020 pandemic again). Gavin and the Kendall Reviews team are keystone supporters of authors and they basically keep my to-read list topped up all year round. For more great recommendations and reading please visit kendallreviews.com.

Content Advisory

These stories feature adult themes including depictions of animal violence, cannibalism, child death, claustrophobia, disordered eating, graphic violence/gore, loss of a loved one, mental health issues, torture, and traumatic death. They may not be suitable for all readers.

INDEX

Copyright	v
Acknowledgments	vii
Content Advisory	ix
Babes Down Boreholes	5
Abstract	25
Parallel	33
White Picket	59
Our Lady of the Trampled Beast	67
Also by BP Gregory	95

Babes Down Boreholes

BP GREGORY

BABES DOWN BOREHOLES

THE COLLAPSE tossed me to the floor. Painful sparks at knee and elbow where I gave up skin to the god of pissed-off caves; not much compared to the colossal *oh shit I'm going to die* that smothered all bandwidth. Terror devolved me right down to a tender worm beneath the descending boot and I jacknifed into a c, then an s, shredding my ass trying to burrow into hard stone and hide.

The bit you'd call the actual disaster was over in a New York minute. A seismograph needle tripping the groove, or perhaps that was the thin unsavoury air talking. The aftermath stretched slow and dreamy as a melting record groaning out sad songs, bad songs, songs to break up to as they drip in tarry honey down the turnstile.

The subterranean roar that was shattering my bravery swiftly became grumbling. Then the grumbling wandered off like some drunk old uncle, away through the walls. I was left lying stunned and alone with my tinnitus shrieking *eeee*, excitedly trying to tell me something had happened.

Oh, and it turned out my eyes weren't squeezed shut in fright after all. The torch had gone "pop!" and bye-bye when I dropped it in the excitement. The rockfall had stranded me in perfect darkness.

Tentatively, in case I made things worse (my speciality), I wobbled up onto all fours. Just my arms shaking now, not the world, good, good. What was that godawful taste? I spat out a big drooly mess of limestone foam. I was dusted all over like an expensive biscuit with a miraculous fuzz of grit — miraculous, as it could've been boulders with just a fingernail's less luck.

'Let's … let's give it a second,' I wheezed.

Suffice to say the tunnel floor was a disorienting place. You don't spend a lot of time on the ground as an adult, not if things are going well. Expensive paper crackled in my left fist as I moved; likely my panic-convulsion had compressed it into a sweaty diamond. I must still be clutching Doctor Wise's letter like a talisman.

Wasn't like I hadn't already wasted too many evenings reading every damn line of the good Doctor's summons, right from the moment it arrived.

Standing in my musty hall, made dull by sleet's insistent rapping at the pane. Curling violet toes. All of my socks were more hole than sock, exposing my little piggies to the cruellest of elements.

Sorting the usual barrage of envelopes marked *overdue* and the frankly aggressive *there shall be no further warning* which even now provoked faint dread; before coming upon Wise's letter like a bolt from the blue, straight through the mail slot and into my heart.

I tore it open on the spot, icy feet be damned. Hands definitely not trembling, although I suspected the heat off my face could fry a British breakfast. Glad nobody else was in at this hour to laugh. Only little ol' me, marooned in this leaky house, keeping company with the choices that'd caused my falling out of step with the world.

My inner cynic whispered, *'Just another bill coming due,'* but honestly he was more into being clever than helpful and could sod right off. I rapidly checked the letter front and back in case "I miss you" was hidden and I'd somehow skipped past in my eagerness. Perhaps encoded in Wise's "dire mystery" "primeval tunnel" "you must witness" hyperbole that was every bit as purple as my overgrown toenails.

I always felt behind the eight ball with Doctor Wise. It had taken a long time and a lot of soul searching to realise this was done in deliberate poor faith, as part of his cultivated mystique. What can I say? The lure of older men. The catnip was as effective on my poor self-esteem as on the purse strings of funding bodies, who love to be humiliated.

Even knowing this, I turned the envelope inside-out to check — really, nothing? Not a scribble? — in case anyone's wondering how big a schmuck I actually am. In lieu of sweet nothings my old flame had enclosed a sheaf of pinks (a.k.a. allied military currency, allied to our side of course), the bills so crisp they might've been freshly printed.

My embarrassment that he'd correctly assumed the bus and boat of his requested journey beyond my means (and thank fuck my passport hadn't expired) didn't lessen my superstitious dread that it was terrible luck to handle pinks. After all, they'd hardly keep cranking them out if the war were as put to bed as the beaming newscasters assured every night at six. And anyone with eyes in their head could watch how those televised cheeks pulling up into grins, exhorting us to be joyful, were themselves shrinking to showcase tendon and tooth.

Witnesses were due home any minute and I hastily stuffed the incriminating scrip and more importantly the letter into my pocket before my roommates could see. Sure, nursing me back from tragedy had grown old. They could hardly be sicker of it than me.

They'd loudly demand a trip to market courtesy of the pinks; fish, maybe even a taste of meat! Then off to Sammy's for a few eye-watering rounds of whatever his bathtub was brewing. And they wouldn't be wrong, that's what any sane soul would do. The cheery clink of glasses: fuck my fallen trajectory, fuck the high and mighty Doctor, and most of all fuck love, hey?

I finally got my composure under wraps just as the house's other denizens piled in the door. Shouting, crowding the hallway with damp wool and bags. At the last moment I noticed my fingers were festive with bright pink stains. A fresh print indeed.

A sudden moment of panic, greeting morphed into the only excuse I could think of, one of unstable bowels. Dignity out the window as jeers chased me to the tiny bathroom. With my hands stinging under chill water I had to scrub, and scrub, and scrub.

◀

Poured over me, the mountain's clotted darkness was so thick it was like my stupid eyes had fallen out. My occipital lobe, currently my least-favourite lobe, kept throwing out bursts of ghostly jellyfish to amuse itself. This managed to spook me and was overall as unhelpful as possible.

Concussion could make it do that. If I'd been bonked during the cave-in I'd *like* to think I'd have noticed, but honestly on a day when everything was runny and sliding downhill who could say. No pain, beyond the general (those sad, sad songs, even underground). Fingers crept through my scalp and reported only thinning vanity, no damp or spongy bits.

Which was more than could be said for my rapidly cooling trousers. If avoiding my housemates had previously sent my pride over the windowsill, it was now exiting the stratosphere. And I had to question, in a rush of helplessness that left my knees weak, what exactly I'd planned had my hand encountered hot brain spilling across my shoulders? Pat it and say, "There, there?"

'There, there,' I whispered comfortingly. Things weren't so bad in the balance. I was still here. I swiped powdered mica from my cheeks; and right now I probably looked like some sparkly subterranean unicorn, so there was that.

While I'd been gnawing the pointless old bone of worry it was worth noting that the cave was industriously sucking the heat right from my marrow to keep for itself. So at least one of us was achieving. Glad as I was in all my worst moments for no witnesses, I mentally and physically pulled my socks up. I got moving, and crawled until I bumped my nose (ow).

My new friend Mr Wall was handy for helping me get back on my feet. Thanks wall. No thanks to you, rest of the cave; my teeth wouldn't stop chattering.

'Uh … hello?' Marshalling courage I called into the void, becoming more confident with the second one. 'Hello!'

Flat judgmental silence.

If there were others from Doctor Wise's group nearby, shaken but not stirred like me, they weren't answering. Typical.

Or perhaps a *teensy* bit my fault: I'd been drifting off from the fray prior to the collapse. Too obsessed over which babe in the woods of this year's intake had caught the Doctor's eye.

Honestly if it weren't for the lack of sight, the trembling uncertainty, and the rock dust gritting my teeth I'd be kind of pleased to have landed on my own. Constantly weighing my appeal against the others, their every whiffle and fart, had worn me down even over the brief time we'd been out here. I'd already been daydreaming of putting my ass right back on that goddamned boat, even it almost killed me the first time.

So which way freedom? I couldn't boast a rich history of successful decisions; it'd been too easy to drift where the tides flowed. Adored, and then so suddenly discarded; not that the incident impeded Doctor Wise's career in any way. A whiff of scandal only made him titillating at parties. The cherry on top was to have obediently toddled out here and stuffed myself down this crack in a mountain at the tail end of nowhere, all for want of a bit of personal initiative.

Wise had known I would come. Of a sudden all I wanted was to smash his smug face right through this rough wall that I clung to in my private abyss. Friend Wall and I, we could do it together.

'Fuck it. I'm heading left,' I said out loud. 'Because I want to.'

In imagination, my roommates cheered wildly. So vividly that I could almost taste that mangy sock stank that accompanied them everywhere. I immediately felt better. Or if not better, than vindicated, which was the next best thing.

Keeping one hand on the rock (I love you Wall) I began shuffling along my chosen route toward escape. Every day I'm shufflin'. Trying not to let recollections of famous past cave rescues freeze me to the spot: babies down boreholes and other, stickier ends. I doubted I'd be Winnie the Poohing my way out like sweet baby Jessica singing to herself in the dark.

And I for sure lacked the popularity of poor Floyd Collins. To the end he'd wept for his hordes of fans not to leave him, as high above his head they'd picnicked in the bright sun, mussing their Sunday best.

If what the woman back at the hostel had confided about this cave was true, well. Let's not think too hard about that, shall we?

Us Wise acolytes had been the sole guests converging on the isolated hostel. Buried in bracken halfway up the mountain, the spot couldn't have boasted eager throngs even back when nature was a legitimate hobby, instead of an excuse to get pegged by some AWOL sniper.

For me the transcontinental journey had passed like a fever dream. The bone-rattling tedium was only leavened by the prospect of seeing *him* again and I kept his letter in my pocket as comfort against the unfamiliar tastes and smells. It wasn't a great sign that I'd reverted to thinking of Doctor Wise as "him," as though his name were too much to bear. Old habits die hard.

Not even my sulky self-absorption could ignore the mountains, though. Having such huge edifices of rock chopping up the skyline does something unsettling to your thoughts, so that you gasp at the sight, trail off. The others would have thought me such a flake if we weren't all guilty of doing it. "Welcome to Vague Mountain" was a running joke. No doubt we were of a type. Not a nice feeling to realise you're a "type," the same gullible faces staring back innocently.

As we tromped into the hostel the sight of ripped lagging and exposed pipes made me suspect they'd ridden out the lockdown, as so many did, by billeting soldiers. I was quietly smug at not turning up dainty nostrils like *some* horrified members of our party.

We descended on Doctor Wise in the communal dining room where he rose, pipe in hand, with a welcoming smile. Even recognising the set piece I'd thought I'd never smell that woodsy tobacco again, and was so overwhelmed that I almost publicly broke down right there.

Despite my insomniac agonies of the past couple of days I received no secret signal or gesture from the Doctor. Humility kicked me to the back of the group like a genuine ass. Truly I was one among many. I clutched my letter and looked for anything else to do.

A woman manned a bain-marie near the kitchen, enveloped in bleach-scented steam as she lifted each lid. By her scowl she was clearly stationed to stem greed, rather than in any gesture toward service. As she spooned out my pittance of boiled carrots she pursed her lips unhappily. 'Won't catch me messing around no cave. Not for any money.'

I looked down. Bounty from some luckier country, that had weathered the conflict well enough to grow and can these neon vegetables. With the resources to send them halfway around the world to be scattered on my plate like babies' thumbs.

Miss Bain-Marie sported the same brittle locks and chafed complexion as everyone. Still, it felt nice to be chatted to — I'd rapidly unearthed the nothing I had in common with the rest of the team. I'd also been trialling a beard, which covered a few sins. Maybe she found me charming. 'We're not getting paid to go. You wouldn't fancy coming on a stroll, then?'

She ignored that. 'Locals call that cave a keeper.'

Of course my traitor eyes flicked to where Wise lorded over the communal table. Bollocks-deep in supplicants. 'Why? Nobody wants to share it?'

Her flaking lips made that moue again. She took back a baby thumb as a penalty. 'It means once you get lost in there nobody from around here's coming to retrieve your body.

It's just too hard, that cave.'

Well. Didn't I feel like a dickhead. If you were into foreshadowing, call that the first poor omen.

I locked the bathroom door that night and shaved my beard. The Doctor hadn't noticed it anyway.

Following its solid start, my great cave escape wasn't coming up roses. The hair all across my skin prickled like itchy radars, trying to work out what was out there in the dark. Now that eyes no longer kept them in line my hands and feet had taken the opportunity to bloat into balloon things that kept wobbling about. Plenty to run into.

'Stalactites and stalagmites,' I sang, falsetto, into the ink. With the guidebook long gone I'd little idea of what distinguished one mineral formation from another — you could crash into any of them and take a layer of skin off. Skinners, they should have called them. Classified entirely by how much of a bite they could take. 'Stalagmites and stalactites.' The ditty ended in a hysterical titter that warned me I needed to put a cork in that shit right now.

The fluid of my inner ears, that mysterious sea, sloshed nauseatingly at being cut free from any reference ... bar Walls McRocks here. And who knew where the fuck he was taking me. So yeah. Not going great.

To stave off panic I occasionally stood quiet and still. If I held my breath I fancied I caught far off coughing or muttering. Other lost Wise sheep wandering their own course, or lying pinned scratching weakly at rubble. Difficult to bristle my quills at these so-called competitors now: we could all hear each other, and nobody could reach anyone.

Choices. Left or right. Trail the venerable Doctor to a bar following his lecture, or wander home. Listen to his diatribe as the rosé rises, let's face it rather unflatteringly, in his complexion. Oh but right then at the start you'd felt so *special*. So on course.

Pained, hitched sobbing echoed in the tunnel, battled with itself. The kind that's jerked out of you in bloody gobbets. Christ, kid, I thought, get a grip. Or perhaps that was my voice and somebody else was tuning in judgmentally. My roommates went through months of this, and it occurred that when I got home I was very much going to owe them a beer.

Bleach stung my nostrils and every nerve quickly sprang rigid with horrible electricity. That smell had no business being down here in the dark. Saint Bain-Marie sighed, stirring hidden currents of air. She shook her head right by my ear so that lank tresses tickled the side of my face, and slurred, 'Nobody's coming. Keeper.'

I shrieked and swung my arms, encountering nothing. I hoped for nothing more than the mountain to crush me so that this would stop.

▶

Team Wise clustered about the cave entrance in the thin sunshine, jiggling to restore circulation and just gosh darn excited to be off the bus. I thought we resembled a pack of schoolies more than the keenest minds of our country hunting revelation. According to Wise's letter we were about to shake the world in its boots.

Hell. What if some of this lot *were* actually kids, they looked young enough. Charismatic Wise would finally be headed for jail or hotter points beyond. I doubted it, though; the Doctor wasn't one to expose himself to genuine risk.

He had keen facility for scenting the loner, the lame. Those whose friends weren't close enough to send up red smoke when he finally showed his nicotine stained teeth, or rich enough to protest when the faculty swept you quietly under the rug.

Doctor Wise scraped vines back to proudly exhibit his discovery, and even I was pulled forward into the ooh-ing scrum. The word GATE looked like it'd been daubed on the rock by something nastier than hands. Scratchier. Cruel bone fingertips came to mind, with beads of pink-stained lymph slipping down the loose skin of a sallow forearm.

I could see them so clearly, like they were coming for my face. Gooseflesh sprang up all over, and I mean *all* over. Even my anus was deeply unnerved. I guess the painting could be considered our second bad sign. Seeing it was the moment I started suspecting this to be a less than stellar idea — for reasons beyond my bruised heart and gravel-rash humiliation.

In my defence, out of our gathering of supposedly bright sparks not a single voice piped up to inquire how the Doctor had found the glyph way out here. He looked as chuffed as if he'd painted it himself. For all we knew maybe he had.

Having peeked behind the curtain (and beneath the sheet) I had to admit that the stars in my eyes had somewhat dimmed. Nonetheless when Wise puffed up his pigeon chest and led us into the mountain like some off-brand Pied Piper I followed at the tail of the gaggle. My best excuse was that slinking back to the bus alone wasn't an alluring prospect.

Sharp, unforgiving surfaces. The underground world was made up of angles whose only purpose was to cut me, or trip, or bounce my skull off them with a hollow "bonk!" that sent stars across my vision. My non-vision.

Shivering gave up the ghost for long periods of smooth frictionless time, then surprise! It hit in violent spasms that rattled me through the rocks like a pinball.

Illusionary or not, the whispers and clicks of the rest of my party had long since vanished. The highlight of my trudge to date was encountering a stretch of wall (I'd decided to call him Fuck You Von Wallerston) that compressed when I pressed in. A rich pond smell I knew from the pottery class I'd joined at the beginning of my studies to fill the long evenings (and that was where I eventually hooked up with my roommates, so never let it be said you can't make new friends).

I scooped clay from Fuck You Von Wallerston, squeezing it into long slick worms. On a whim one got itself flattened beneath my boot. 'Bam!' I grunted. Did it whip into a c or an s, trying futilely to escape? Swallowing the worms eased the cramps and loneliness. For a bit.

High above our heads the occasional flashlight beam flickered uneasily across the ceiling, which rippled with small leathery bodies.

Somewhere up front the short lad with fluffy locks was pissing on about not trampling fragile underground ecosystems. This was hilarious to the rest of us as we waded through guano clutching our noses. Every sinus wept appalled tears of blood.

I was afraid my sense of taste was never going to recover, which would make boiled carrots my last happy memory. A few bats were disturbed into flight, squeaking unhappily at our invasion. They whipped around the big cavern, frenetic loops that in bat lingo might spell *Get out of our bedroom, perverts!*

The aerial acrobatics had us ducking and weaving as we crossed the cavern, arms above our heads so as not to get crapped on. Because we were looking up we all saw it. I wasn't the first to scream and I wasn't the loudest, either.

A pale muscular tentacle uncoiled from the overcrowded ceiling and wham! Snake: one, rodent: zero. It snatched the poor doomed bat from the air mid-flap, no time to even squeak a final *I love you* to its bat babies. A crushing embrace of coils and working jaw.

Roused by our shouting the whole damn colony burst into the air. They were done with our shit. The screeching bat blizzard streamed out through the bright iris of the entrance.

We sprinted the other way, slipping and sliding with torches flailing madly. It was like trying to find the exit at a rave. Curly locks' feet went right out from under him which was literally the worst thing I could imagine (at the time; now we know better, don't we). I hauled him up without stopping and man, that runny acidic goo was all over the kid. I got to admire what it looked like for someone to jog and gag at the same time. Truly this was a journey of wonder.

Gradually our group straggled to a gasping halt deeper within the mountain. Solid ground instead of drizzling slime underfoot, which meant we'd passed beyond casual reach of the surface. Now that panic wasn't whirring around our heads, we took a moment to recover. Who would have thought catching one's breath without a bat up your nose would be a luxury?

And yeah. From a certain point of view, señor cave snake could be counted as our third and final warning.

'So,' a wobbly voice piped up, breaking the sheepish interlude. All torches swung that way and whatshername with the dicky knees blinked in the glare. 'Do we dress up to fight crime now or what?'

That cracked us all up, even Wise who couldn't possibly have caught a pop culture joke.

'Hey, did you hear that?'

'Hear what?'
'A whisper. I swear.'
'Sure, you whispered. Right then.'

Cackling and digging each other in the ribs. A necessary release of tension so that we didn't loose the tears that glimmered in more than one set of eyes. Look at us, ma, we're on an adventure!

Being furthest down the tunnel I also thought I'd caught something. A sound now masked by general tomfoolery. It'd been a sort of ... clicking, or scratching, as of hard fingers. Deliberate and measured.

My imagination immediately flashed to the mountain spirits who were rumoured to have once knocked in cramped dark tunnels (*just like this one!*) to warn ye olde miners of imminent disaster.

Although as humanity loves its villains twice to its saints, there were those who claimed the lurkers sent their *tap tap tap* for more malign reasons. And any prospector who claimed to hear them ought to be shunned by decent folk, which back in the day probably meant getting served last at the bar. Quite the cross to bear.

Smiling, out of habit I turned to share this jest with Wise. Folklore had been our common passion; it marked the only times he hadn't been impatiently waiting his turn to orate. And I saw that the Doctor had heard it too. The look on his face turned my sweat to greasy ice.

He opened his mouth, pale lips quivering. Torch lit from below like a haunted house spook, although I think that was by accident. Too scared for theatrics this time.

I made an instinctive gesture of comfort. The others were still obliviously chattering, loud and brash. I think Doctor Wise said, '... can't get through.'

But I guess I'll never know.

The walls bellowed. The mountain descended to crush us into paste.

◀

Given all we'd gone through together it sure was swell of my buddy Francis St Wall to support my aching spine. Even with the rest of me puddled in a heap at his base. Funny, you know, how things only seem real when they're solid and you can touch them.

I'd given up on understanding the rest of the formless world. And when it wasn't swinging wildly it crouched just out of reach waiting to see what I'd do next.

Not a lot of flesh left on my groping fingers. The tips clicked against my teeth when I put them in my clay-slick mouth. They cut my lip. Even with how exhausted I was, this sent distant waves of revulsion crashing through me. I'd have puked if the worms weren't sitting so heavy and cold at my core, binding me to the stone.

Giving it some old-school determination I managed to get a chunk of rock into my palm. Awkward, leaning back, with the last dregs of strength I began knocking on the wall. *Tappity tap tap*. Make it jaunty. Why not. And when I couldn't hold the rock any longer I just screwed up my face and used my clattering fingers.

I knocked in the hope that somebody might hear and join me here in the dark. I was craving that, you see. And if nobody came, still I rapped out the rhythm of happier times. Even though in the moment I'd not recognised them as such.

The rattle of sleet on glass. Tap tap. Wintery blue light, and the prospect of nothing more exciting than warm socks and a cup of tea to pass the afternoon. It was ok if nobody came. Really. The tapping of my bloodied, overwrought heart slowed, slowed toward some kind of resolution.

ABSTRACT
bp gregory

ABSTRACT

Whoo a gust of foetid breath puffed from the gaping city loop tunnel to swirl and disperse about the larger space, pushed by what was coming. Definitely a bit of a morning whiff, that, not midnight breath. An *"all the beer's dry 'an me toothbrush's arsed"* aroma. Just enough to make Randal gag quietly into his cupped palm. Faint and sick.

Desperate for a wee, too. Too much coffee. Meanwhile his inflamed eyes went all around, checking, assessing. Picking nervously at an incipient subterranean claustrophobia. Paranoid that his solid paunch was somehow expanding to fill the subway.

It was dread, you see. Pure skin-peeling dread and Randal needed to be brave like he'd never been.

No strangers graced the platform. Like fate. Obviously in this day and age with nobody's word worth much there'd be cameras, but how would they identify him snugged up in a hoodie like any unkempt hooligan.

Made our Randal appear, or more so, the sort of fellow that nice ladies crossed the street to avoid. God help him he did love to see 'em scurry away, frail ankles flashing like bunny tails. Didn't make one *feel* any nicer, like, in himself but something was something, hey?

Not five steps distant and turned away into the wind, Broncs had obligingly worn a brimmed hat, hiding his own collapsed face. Fate indeed. Broncs only ventured abroad after dark when there were few to witness. Tantalisingly suspicious … but still, *old folk need less zs than the rest of us* the literature claimed, or at least the digital abstracts that were free to read.

Well lucky fucking him. Randal scowled, rubbing at eggplant varicose. He was eternally flattening out beneath exhaustion. His arms and legs weren't proper limbs, they weighed like numb kettlebells, had to be lugged about.

He usually lost Broncs after the first hour. Not paying enough mind. Mind, you try monitoring a tortoise shuffling about town all night without resting your throbbing brain a second. And doing it dressed as some prat kid besides.

But the online data on Broncs proved anaemic, no matter how diligently massaged. Eventually he'd been forced to dog those hesitant aged steps, which he liked a lot less than his comfy chair.

Randal did wonder if anybody was likely to access his flat full of notes someday, read the hints so painstakingly scraped together. He thought not. Not having watched his landlord heaving the previous tenant's belongings into the dumpster out the back.

When he'd asked where his predecessor had got to, got a disinterested shrug. Junk. That's all these young lads were. Thousands more where they crept from. Not contributing.

ABSTRACT

Hey, not even procreating; wasn't like any broad in her right mind would touch 'em.

Well, Randal thought, breathing hard, getting a bit excited. He was bloody contributing now!

After moving in, it had only slowly dawned that he was in fact subsisting in a flat right beneath General Fucking Broncawei. But once it had, every creak and shudder of the ceiling became especially ominous.

It was on the twentieth anniversary of the trials when the light began to flicker on in the dim brown haze of Randal's thoughts. The same photographs paraded same time every year, exhorting the public, "*War Criminal Still At Large!*" Broadcast to a world that had already wearied, moved on. Likely what the old bugger was counting on.

An atrocity from the dawn of time. Almost before Randal was born. In a country that nobody of these parts spared a blink for, even when it had gone up in flames. Why should they? They had movies and shops and chips with friends on the beach. Hot sun, and shell grit in their smiling teeth.

Only somebody lacking those social gifts would notice.

One hundred and fifty, that's what he'd read. People could only ever care about a hundred and fifty others out of the population of the world; because once upon an age that was the size of your standard tribe. Hardwired in, wasn't it.

Randal's boss had thought him quite the la di dah for trotting out that gem of trivia in the loading dock. The attention was nice, although in the abstract Randal never managed to dig into the nuts and bolts of anything, never understood *why*.

'You and me, old man,' he muttered at Broncs' humped back while gusts of subway air grew fierce. 'You're my hundred fifty.'

A part of Randal was already looking forward to getting this over with. Psyching himself up had left him sick all week:

squats on the loo best not mentioned, the flat viewed through a sort of headachy nausea. He had promised himself a quiet eve with a pizza after.

Numbnuts, he chided, jittery. *Then what'll you do with yourself?* Old Broncs was all that got him out of bed of a morning. Two more anniversaries of the trials had dragged by already while he dithered. But this was the third. It'd all gone on too long, right? And he was *quite* sure he had his man, based on those photos. *Mostly* sure. Felt the truth, he did, in the cockles of his heart.

General Broncawei. The fucking bogeyman. Why ought humble Randal of all folk have been the one to discover him, let alone care? Truly he didn't give two short shits about what that wheezing, coughing old fart hidden away upstairs had done in his heyday. Doubtful you got on the news like that for being a saint.

Nope. Randal was knee deep in this, wiping sweaty palms on his trousers because *Randal* had never been allowed to get away with any damned thing. Not once in his life.

Nothing but job, rent, washing, chores … The sort of existence that made a grown fellow wonder *this isn't at all what I was promised. How did this happen?* He frequently and fervently wished he didn't have to bother his weary skull on it anymore.

So stop bothering, then. Purity of the hunt and all that. This was Randal's moment, his big one, and another wouldn't likely come. Make it last.

The steely wail of the incoming train. *Dopplered*, that was it, 'though he couldn't recall how it worked.

It was now. Randal tugged the cords of his hoodie for luck. Sneakers silent on the platform's pebbled surface — sneaking, ha! Arms outstretched, rigid to push. Flabby, that, throw your weight behind it son. Make it count for something.

He stumbled; oh Randal you've fucked it up! Momentum carrying him on. And there was shrieking, brakes, all the world shrieking, pots and pans and cymbals pummelling his ears. In the throes of it all an iron-hard hand locked onto his arm.

How ironic. Broncs was going to save him.

To the old bastard plump clumsy Randal must have seemed to spring out of nowhere. So was it mere startlement that made the General's seamed lips, so uncomfortably close as Randal swooped by, seem to peel back in feral satisfaction?

Fresh impetus as the hand thrust him forth. Sudden and shocking.

Last but also least, a plaintive thought whimpered in the dark of the tunnel: …

Ha. No time to bother about that anymore.

Parallel

BP GREGORY

PARALLEL

'Ben. Seriously, love. Let me in.'

Bet your bottom dollar the neighbours were only pretending to sleep; holding their breath like naughty children in a game where I wasn't freezing my tits off out here in the hall. The gothic titillation of being Ben's dearly departed scratching for admittance in the (ahem) dead of night wasn't lost on me. Rather keen to get inside before I ended up on someone's social media, to be honest.

Identical spot-lit cream doors, *locked* doors, demanded vertigo as they marched off down the frigid corridor and rounded the bend. My thoughts were too one-dimensional to be coping with this. Any of it. Struggling to stay upright and cling to dignity a while longer, I leaned my inflamed head on the wall.

'They kept me in Immigration for six fucking hours, Ben. I'm *tired*.'

Six hours wasted because how was any sane person supposed to sit in one of those help-yourself-to-my-anus paper gowns through a slideshow on what (not) to do after getting yanked into a parallel world, one where the original you wound up cooling her heels at the morgue. I was hardly going to swan out chortling, 'Gee, that's cleared that up!'

Six hours. Trickling away. Finally; and in line with my growing sarcasm; Immigration decided it'd be just as productive to dump me in the deep end. Which I applauded (sarcastically). Not supposing for a bare second I might sprout gills, mind — I just wanted out.

Since we're counting it's been forty-nine excruciating hours since some poor cleaner stumbled upon, and vomited on, the murder victim. I'd bet forensics hate that, but I could hardly fault Sir Dustalot. I'll spend the rest of my wretched life regretting so much as glancing at the crime scene photos. There's just no way to *un*-see all that a skin's meant to wrap and protect oozing freely into what looks like a very nice antique rug.

Except ... in this weird unnatural parallel place there'd been *two* murders. The boy, plus me. Now I'd swear blind there'd been only one, just *he*. We'd have irrefutable proof if smartphones could be shanghaied from their proper timeline along with people (nope: I arrived as naked as a flabby Terminator). 'Here, there are two victims,' Immigration assured me and then coughed to lower their tone, still inappropriately gleeful at their cleverness in getting me here.

So of course I bloody well hot-footed it home the moment they turned me loose. All of this added up to the nine longest hours of my husband's life. He had to stand in this exact doorway and hear, 'Sir, your wife's been found. I'm afraid it's bad news. I'm afraid it's *murder*,' from officers with basset hound eyes, fiddling with their caps as they discharged the worst part of their job.

Pressed to either side of this wall, Ben and I were shackled to the same impossible hope. That the lost aren't really gone, and it was all a horrible joke.

I banged my forehead in frustration, and listened to the rapt peanut gallery of neighbours listening to me tap-tapping at Ben's chamber door. The latch eventually rattled, thank fuck; my knees were crapping out. My spouse's familiar features tentatively peeked around the frame. Even distorted by that haunted puffy stare, Ben's face let me believe, ever so briefly, that this might still be ok.

Friends and other critics have quipped that my dear spouse bears a striking similarity to Satan. Plying his nights as a head chef, some real A Night On Bald Mountain stuff as that purgatorial kitchen revolves around him. Revealed in slices by the apartment door, the lord of darkness appeared to have collapsed in on himself.

Now, I can't go tossing glitter in the air and claiming to have the perfect marriage. Nonetheless my heart seized like a shitty old blender on seeing what my death had done to the big man. *Her* death, rather.

'Keep that line between realities straight,' the Immigration mooks had said, a whole slide devoted to it. She: dead, me: alive. They definitely hadn't figured on me running *wee wee wee* all the way home.

Well fuck Immigration sideways. Their advice was utterly trivial against the sweet cedar of Ben's aftershave as he sobbed into my neck.

The cream hall's expectant hush sank away to join my other flatline memories as I trailed Ben into our apartment, slamming the door with a flourish. Take that, nosy neighbours. Why don't you whine about it at the next committee meeting?

Ben kept trying to fit himself against me in odd, abortive ways, as though my right arm wasn't there. All the while pointedly not glaring at my two hands like I'd sprouted an extra head. Here, his wife had been short a limb from birth. Immigration kōan: how do you miss something that never existed.

Sooner than you'd think I'd had enough of this, and I shoved my kind, funny, diabolical husband away across the bed. Her widower. This was not working out how I'd hoped: Ben's grief was so smothering that it left no air to figure out how I felt. He filled the room; my nerves were too clogged with him.

I left Ben hunched mutely with those chopping block mitts over his appalled mouth. Would have apologised if I could work out what the dead were supposed to say. Instead I padded into the study for a gasp of fresh air; and, if I were being honest, to see what breadcrumbs my shadow-self had left.

I cleared my throat and mused aloud to the bleeding darkness of the bedroom doorway, just to be speaking. Bring normalcy in by the scruff. 'Looks like she got her private eye license at the same time I did.' Slapped it proudly up on the wall in a cheap frame, the kind you get at the post office. I wondered if her classmates had been as thoroughly intolerable as mine.

'Huh.' Flipping through papers, 'Kept the bread and butter work up better than me, too. Good on her.' More pennies in the bank meant she missed Ben stomping from room to room flipping off lights and loudly declaring money doesn't grow on trees you know. Perhaps a disloyal thought with my own private Lucifer going to pieces in the next room, but people are only as good as themselves.

Morbid curiosity made me peer between wall and desk. The plaster was dotted like a tiny moonscape with the desiccated lumps and curls of a booger stash. Yep, my worst habit. My lost twin clearly wasn't different enough, or was in the wrong sorts of ways, to have left easy answers here.

My search was interrupted by red and blue lights which skittered beneath the curtain and began crawling up the walls. No mistaking those *uh oh you're in trouble* colours. Shuddering out of my fugue I padded over to peer shiftily into the street without disturbing the curtain, only realising I was acting guilty once I'd done so. In the mindset of hunkering down to hide already, becoming small. That's what going home did to you.

One of those massively schnozzed police wagons was gliding to a stop at the kerb outside. Huh. So that's how they wanted to play it.

Would've been nice to have time to get changed first: my Immigration-issued tracksuit and slip-ons made me look on day release, a slippery bit of psychology on their part. Obviously I wasn't ready to assume the other me's clothes yet. Seemed a bit intimate for day one.

Not to mention that if I *did* go there, I'd likely have to replace most of her custom tailored tops. Given the overstuffed wardrobe, no prize for guessing where she'd sunk her extra pennies — it'd probably be cheaper to saw my own arm off.

Ben still lurked in the still water of the darkened bedroom. I saw little point in tiptoeing shamefully out, or, at the other end of the spectrum, shouting goodbye. He could see the police lights for himself. His brimstone breath fogging the window from behind his own curtain.

The night air perked me right up, fresh as a shot of vinegar to the sinuses. Sullen intimation of dawn threatening to give us all something to cry about. Only those whose lives are not right find ourselves up and about at this hour.

Clenching my teeth to avoid chattering, I approached the fuzz wagon through its surreal disco of light. The neighbours would surely bitch to Ben about the disturbance come morning because some folk have no decency. I secretly prayed for him to go full infernal on them. Let's drag the cops back out and do it properly.

The driver's window hummed down, dome light clicked on and I found myself face to face with the improbably named Detective Constable Candi Pensi. Detective Pensi (I steered clear of "Candi") cut a distinctive figure even when she wasn't tunnelling holes through me with her eyes. Her parents can't possibly have suspected they were bringing this disgruntled bear into the world in place of a child, otherwise they'd have named her Brunhilda or Gert.

Pensi was usually spotted up the back of press conferences, maintaining crisp parade readiness as the speaker droned on. I'd seen the occasional greenhorn dare to fidget or chat, only to find Pensi's hand descending on their shoulder like Damocles' sword.

For her sins, among the many other hats of an underfunded service Pensi was attached to cold cases. And just like that I figured out how I'd died. *Detected*, you might say. My first gut reaction was hot fizzing excitement: that's how messed up this was.

The optical death rays continued as I slid meekly into the passenger seat. Once I shut the predawn chill out everything cold started tingling, which was everything.

'I assume you have adequate reason for leaving Immigration and not proceeding directly to the crime scene as agreed.'

'Seriously?'

She cranked the engine with an angry twist. 'Popping across worlds doesn't confer any extra brain cells then.'

'Popping across.' Like the existential horror of my being here was a jaunt for ice-cream.

'However you like to describe it.'

In mutual sullenness we hissed through the empty streets, heading for the nice part of town. Everything glimpsed through the smeary glass renewed my sick misery because it *almost* looked normal. The brief flicker of a neon and skyscraper CBD. A heck of a lot more slums than I was used to. Top heavy wealth distributed in ways that labour couldn't access and decency couldn't halt.

Still, somebody ought to have said no; and I wasn't just chewing over the scenery. I pinned my loathing on Pensi for being in range. 'I still don't get why the Carringtons didn't draw a fresh version of their kid from somewhere.' And leave me be.

A cackle, which wasn't quite the response I'd been shooting for. 'You think you're anyone's top pick?'

Only Ben's, I supposed. And he lacked the obscene means of the ultra-rich to split reality. Ordinary grief was without power, simply spilled out on the floor.

Pensi shifted, kangarooing the suspension. 'The physics of this is way past my pay grade, mind …'

'But?'

'Way I hear it, there's no version where the Carrington boy survived. Not within reach. Poor kid was murdered in every single one.'

Well that left my righteous sails hanging limp. 'All of them?'

Alternate universes exist for every possibility. Sure. Shuffled together like a pack of cards. Only, the shuffle isn't random. *Likelihood* determines how close variations sit, and you can't reach so far from your own card to, say, a world where cheese sandwiches rule instead of humans. It's just too far.

What Pensi was saying was that the murder of the Carrington boy was so perfect it was impossible to undo. Whereas I, who in this universe bled out right there next to him, could be snatched across from my peaceful native existence where I hadn't turned up at the crime scene at all.

She was still going. 'Drove the dowager Carrington into frothing blood. You try telling the fancy folk they can't have something. Which I guess makes you the booby prize. The next best thing to getting her baby boy back.'

'If you're gonna say "revenge," just let me fling myself out into traffic right here.'

'Here you are. The woman who came closest to nabbing the killer.'

'It's the Brunswick Butcher, isn't it.' Hating the way my voice squeaked.

Pensi glanced lazily across; I'd far prefer she watched the road. 'Boils your kettle, does it? *You* never got so close to the Butcher, or you wouldn't be alive and sweating all over my nice clean upholstery. Not much of a private dick.'

'Thanks *Detective*.'

'Calm your tits. This ought to be a walk in the park even for you. All I want is for you to take a gander at the scene and tell me what she knew. How the fuck did the real you manage to interrupt the Butcher in the middle of the fucking murder, basically.'

Seemed pretty obvious. 'She died. That's how.'

Pensi glanced my way again. And grudgingly, because she wasn't a total bitch, she added, 'Forensics reckon she went down trying to save the boy.'

The real me. I stared bleakly through the windscreen. 'What a hero.'

Police spotters still lingered at Carrington House, which could more accurately be called Carrington Mansion seeing as the spaniels enjoyed their own colonnaded entrance. Driving up to the main gate we passed officers with restless eyes. It was depressing how often bad guys couldn't resist sneaking back to gloat.

Pensi wanted me hustled inside, so, stung by the contrary fairy, I lollygagged obnoxiously. If her cool cop friends saw us hanging out so much the better; the force might occasionally work tandem with private-eyes, but only good ones, and it wasn't a loving union.

I had failed to take a proper gander at how the other half lived the last time I stood out here, forty-six hours ago and in the real world. I'd been too busy jostling hip to shoulder with the rest of the parasites, baying for a disgusted security cordon to confirm that the Brunswick Butcher had indeed struck again. Needless to say we got nothing. Right out front of a house where a kid had just died; now, with the luxury of reflection I flushed in shame.

My escort got sick of my tourism real quick. Taking me into physical tow Pensi crunched us down a crushed quartz path onto the grounds. The glittering ribbon rambled among tennis courts, drought-hostile roses and even more water-hungry swimming pools, making sure we'd dutifully admired it all before we reached the house.

I'd dabbled a bit in home security, trying to pin down my calling, and I murmured, 'Good luck getting surveillance.' Even had there been a thousand cameras, you could sneak an elephant through this setup.

Pensi shrugged. 'Dogs might love an intruder to death, at a pinch.' The spaniels had polished our shoes frantically enough before ascertaining that neither visitor was a sausage, after which they'd flocked away.

The motley sideshow of photo-op cops, forensics, coroner and heck-all else had already disbanded from the main house taking whatever they felt they needed. Clearly nowhere near enough, if you asked Mrs Carrington. Which I couldn't. Not without a ticket to the part of Aspens that plebs like me never see. The lofty matriarch who demanded her pound of flesh didn't seem inclined to grapple with me in person, instead leaving Pensi and I to her ... butler, I guess? Was "butler" still a thing?

He certainly buttled out from the soft Parisian green corridors with old-school officiousness. Showed no sign of recognition when we put on our best gravitas and asked to be let in. Back in the real world I'd slipped Captain Buttle three months' wage for a few illicit photographs of the boy's body in the library. So easy these days, he palmed his phone when nobody was looking, snappity-snap. A privacy nightmare.

Not a flicker from him now, of course. A) in this reality we'd never met; b) he didn't equate me with murder victim number two because of the whole arm thing; and c) even if Buttle'd put two and two together he'd need to be a genius, as the Butcher had pulled his signature dick move of making tartare out of human features. My double's face had been erased. I very much hoped they kept that titbit from Ben.

'Please.' Spoken entirely through the nose, posh-style. 'Come inside. We've waited to clean up until after you're finished.'

The library actually wasn't too different to my covert photographs, although I'd never imagined I'd visit in person. Burgundy hardback ranks poised to crash down and squash visitors into ignorant little pancakes. Shiny hardwood floor. The devastated yet still clearly expensive rug. It was smug. Let's call it the smug room.

Two triangles of crisp white, like dropped condolence cards, indicated where corpses had been hauled away. In case you somehow missed the congealed munificence of the black pudding lake. Despite bay windows flung wide to admit genteel eddies of tea rose and chlorine the smell was not amazing.

There was also no dodging the fact that that had been me, there, splayed out with the cleaner's puke in my hair. I gabbled to hide my nerves. 'Is that my blood? If I touch it will the universe implode?'

'For you, yes, because I will shoot you for disrupting a crime scene. Stay where you are by the door. Just tell me what you see.'

'Stay,' I mimicked, sotto voice, like a child. Deeply grateful that the bodies had been carted away and I didn't have to look at myself. The photos of the curled shrimp kid haunted my conscience already, joining the Butcher's other (known) victims whose snapshots got passed around the chat rooms like baseball cards.

Guess that was me tacked onto that list. So what did *her* research unearth that I missed, for her to come waltzing into this smug library and boop the Butcher right on his nose? Not that it did her much good.

I found I couldn't keep my eyes off the blood. Even with the gaping windows the lush room was beginning to press in claustrophobically. An acidy stink crawling backwards down my throat. Squeezing my eyes to keep tears private I carefully edged down to rest on the floor, just in case damsel-esque swooning was something that happened in real life.

'Anything?'

I shook my head, not trusting words.

Pensi's colossal *my fucking day* sigh was anything but sympathetic. She was probably supposed to be working a hundred other cases as well as messing around with this shit. 'Why was someone like you "investigating" the Butcher in the first place?' Air quotes. The lighter side of sarcasm.

'Haven't you heard? Hobbies are essential for good mental health.'

'Fuck right off. What kind of hobby is that?'

'My class all set ourselves assignments …'

'Your fake-ass detective class, you mean.'

Given today, I had to strain for offense. Bless Pensi for trying, though. 'We took on a pet project each, sort of like a competition. Dig into our favourite cold cases, and of course everyone chose locals. The Gelato Van Poisoner, the Flemington Bridge Flayer. The Brunswick Butcher. And then we kind of stuck with them after we graduated.' Like a club, I didn't want to say because that made us sound morbid.

'Like a goddamn murder club.' Fair enough.

Chasing a sniff of the glamour that'd lured us to "information services" in the first place. We'd too quickly found that the actual work typically involved slumping in your car feeling vertebrae fuse and watching an endless succession of windows. Some light digging through trash, like a professional raccoon. It was a shameful statistic of mine that none of my cases ever got so far as court.

Pensi sniffed. 'It's a bit hard to go calling the Butcher a "cold case" now.'

'It was hardly ever cold; just nobody gave two shits about the sort of people he killed. That's why he targeted them. I mean, look at this song and dance, all around some rich white kid.' It certainly wasn't about me and I'd lain there just as dead.

Pensi's face went red with anger. 'I give two shits, alright? You would not believe the size of the shits I give. But you're right, I think he's escalating. Picking riskier targets.'

'He thinks nobody can catch him.'

Her mouth twisted like she'd bitten into a dead rat. She'd had to stand with her thumb up her ass while the Carringtons blew their fortune on insane physics violations instead of, say, funding a proper taskforce. Meanwhile politicians screamed for the police to arrest all the monsters and jaywalkers at once, slap a nice bow on it. 'I want your research. All of it.'

'My fake-ass detective research.' Suddenly, overwhelmingly tired, like my bones had been injected with lead. 'Fine.'

'Get off the floor and get out of here. Here, you take my card, and you call if you suddenly become useful.'

Pensi hesitated, balancing a grain of decency against having places to be. I must have looked incredibly pathetic.

'Want a ride home?'

'Actually, can you spot me a couple of bucks?'

I picked a shabby motel because Pensi's charity only stretched so far, and mission brown was such a classic self-punishment. Unwilling to touch my double's clothes or husband, I sure as heck wasn't ready to dip sticky fingers into her life savings.

Fortunately this wasn't some wacky universe where x won the war instead of y, and we were consequently all using some mad currency I couldn't get my head around, like goats. The only thing significantly different here was me. It was like the worst episode of Star Trek I'd ever heard of.

A bright new day beamed in through the curtains, which made me want to hide from its obnoxious cheer. Just let me collapse and spend some quality time unconscious. Instead I slumped on the dusty coverlet, freeing a sprinkle of moths, and hoisted the landline to dial the last person I wanted to deal with. Whether my spouse or hers, Ben deserved to know what was going on.

'Ben. Hi.'

A rough intake of breath. 'So I wasn't dreaming. Where are you?'

'Motel.'

A long silence. Longer. The cortisone spritzer must be wearing off because I was nodding toward sleep by the time he spoke next. 'Did you help the cops?'

'How, exactly, would I manage that?' Ugh, wind it back.

'Sorry. They figured I might know something that she knew that I didn't, which I don't.'

'Ok.'

'Look, a Constable Pensi's going to swing by to pick up my Butcher files. You can't miss her; she looks like a gym instructor swallowed Sasquatch. Maybe she'll find something they can use.'

'Sure.' He didn't ask if I was coming home, which was a relief. I guess neither of us felt stable enough to crack that wriggling can. I made concluding noises and hung up.

For as long as I could tolerate contact with the yellowed sheets I could lie back and obsess over the Butcher at my leisure. The police were all over it now, so anyone's guess why I couldn't just let it go. So far as I knew nobody from my class had succeeded in making a single bee's dick of difference to any of their cold cases. It hardly felt like I was about to start now.

Having tossed and turned and basted in ancient tobacco stink all day I rose from my pallet at dusk. "Refreshed" would be polishing the turd. Let's claim that I was clear-headed, and better prepared to be practical — I by god didn't want to live out the rest of my life in this motel.

If I intended on dogpaddling through the next few days I'd have to at least dip a toe into my shadow's world. I needed some things from home.

Because nowhere does it specify "bravery" on a private eye application form I hid around the corner to watch Ben leave for work. Being a chef Ben had zero bereavement leave up his sleeve; nonetheless I fumed watching him fold himself into our crappy Datsun. I mean, I *died*. Surely the scalloped potatoes could wait a few nights. But apparently not, because off he went.

Shortly after, the locksmith I'd booked from the motel came ambling up the drive and I trotted out to meet him. I paid with fistfuls of dollars from the swear jar and there was a notable lack of fuss over my lack of ID. Our wedding portrait in the entry likely smoothed the way: Ben and I beaming so wide we looked ready to bite welcoming chunks off whoever chanced the threshold. Perhaps the locksmith just assumed my arm had grown back.

I was finally left alone to beat the bounds of our modest apartment. Hardly the Carrington digs. Pacing neurotically beneath a stucco ceiling where cobwebs snagged and dangled — seriously, didn't we ever look up? I hoped the police hadn't noticed.

Pensi's mates had done a number on the study. The desk looked a bit pathetic with years of notes stripped away, and I wondered if I'd be getting any of it back. Perhaps not wouldn't be such a bad thing. I'd given years of my life, and now look.

Something curious in the bedroom. Not like that, pervert. My ledger was sitting out on the bed in all its shabby glory. The cops were supposed to have scooped up everything relevant to comb through, and were probably taking turns right now reading my faltering deductions in a series of funny voices.

So why had Ben kept this? Was he worried — I mean, *more* worried — about money?

I flipped the last page open, the last entry. Oh.

Inappropriate giggles spilled out as I read. Sounding just as crazed in that cobwebby apartment as you'd expect. This was it. This was how the bitch was different, every bit of it. Ben hadn't circled the address, nothing so obvious; but you don't weather a matrimonial decade without picking up some tips on how your better half thinks. What an asshole I was, assuming he was off to work.

Frantically digging Pensi's card from my pocket I stabbed at the wall phone. Before she'd even lifted the speaker to her ear I was blurting, 'Ben's going after the Butcher!'

Pensi didn't need to take a moment to catch up. I wish I were that cool. 'Why?'

'Because he's a big baby who believes in explanations, happy endings and getting tucked in at night, why do you think? I want police, lots of police, all the police you can send ... can you breed more? Is there time?' Aware that babbling wasn't actually helpful I read out the address from my ledger.

There was an awkwardly loaded pause, as in the same charged moment we both realised who was closer.

'Listen right now, don't you dare head over there. Wait for officers ...'

Sorry Pensi. The dropped handset dangled, barking her orders into the void.

I stumbled outside, somehow managed to locate my feet through tumbling panic and then went pounding across the dusk landscape of letterboxes and lawns. Of course, I immediately found myself jostling with scores of after-work joggers for the lit footpath. Them, seal-slick and almost invisible in lycra against the shadows, grimly pounding out their ten thousand before bed. Me, flapping along in my pyjama-ish Institute tracksuit like I'd slipped away from the kind of place that doesn't allow scissors.

When a bus hissed and sidled up to its stop as I was passing I thought, why not. Wasn't like this could get any more ridiculous. Nary a blink as I staggered aboard. I guess drivers weren't paid to police the respectability of their passengers; they had to go home to stucco like everyone else.

Our steed wallowed along its slow route of rescue, and my fellow travellers stared stoically out the windows. I alone jittered from foot to foot, my heart a bunch of nails shaken in a can.

If a single stranger had thought to touch my arm and ask if I was ok I would have shattered.

Next stop. Come ooon.

Not soon enough I was awkwardly shouldering the accordion door aside in my haste. Got a nice bruise, and numbed my arm to the elbow. The urban gloom had me straining after house numbers because apparently the simple courtesy of streetlights was a stretch out this way. The air was greasy with dinners frying and ordinary lives unwinding.

I actually started sprinting the wrong direction up the road and howled in frustration when I realised. Local mutts took up the chorus from their yards.

I spotted our parked Datsun, with no Ben inside, moments before I saw the neat little weatherboard house I'd been looking for. Blink, and I found myself standing in the buttery porch glow and mashing the doorbell like a maniac.

A young woman answered, looking understandably miffed. Her hair was up in jumbo curlers which I thought only happened in the forties. *Please, please let it be a mistake.* However, 'Oh hello,' she chirped recognising me. 'Do you have an update on the case?' Manners first, and putting your finger on what looked wrong clearly came second in this household.

I opened my mouth, and, '*Where'syourhusband?*' fired out in a breathless gasp.

'Why, the shed office, out back. He's with a visitor though and really doesn't like to be disturbed …'

Oh I'll bet he doesn't. I was already tearing around the side of her picturesque home. I immediately collided with the bins, recycling rolling underfoot. The back yard was a cramped paved oblong, about the best you could expect this close to the city. The shed almost filled it and every shoddy seam bulged with light. I didn't bother knocking.

Jumbled impressions as I burst in, that had to be integrated rapidly if I was to survive the next few seconds. Ben had been tossed to the floor, and I practically piled on top of him. Above us loomed the Brunswick Butcher. And when I say he loomed I know it was only a shed but he scraped the fucking ceiling.

He was the embodiment of every grizzled tradie who's ever stumped across a construction site. Bullish crimson head fastened directly to shoulders. Face a leathery starburst. Hey, would you look at that: literal blood on his hands, spattering to the floor.

The Butcher was wielding a straight razor in one hand and a small gun in the other. I don't know what type, I don't know my guns other than they all go bang in the end. At my entrance the deadly muzzle rose from Ben to jab at me. Great. My cup runneth over. I risked a glance down. Ben's face was gashed, but he had a tiny, brutally sharp paring knife jabbing up at his attacker. Chefs are not a breed to mess with.

Under the gun's eye I could only stand there. I ought to have been jelly and don't get me wrong, my insides had turned to slurry but this asshole thinks he can murder *my husband*. The outraged desire to hook the Butcher's ears and rip his face right off made me rattle and shake.

When I failed to cringe before the penis-substitute of his gun — was that how that worked? — the Butcher's wrinkly face clenched in displeasure. Honestly it was like watching a cat's bum pinch off. Although I knew punishment was coming quick-sticks I couldn't suppress a little snork of amusement. Fervently hoped that getting up his nose was how I'd died the first time.

Here we go.

Then the Brunswick Butcher glimpsed an issue more pressing over my shoulder, through the open door I'd crashed through. I didn't dare turn to look. The grimace the monster flashed me was a pledge, was death, and I peed myself a smidgin right there.

Time felt like it had frozen as he folded his hand around the razor and reached out one gnarled, dripping finger. All my muscles screamed at me to move, fat lot of good that it did. I finally understood the uselessness of a rabbit in headlights just before the splat. The despair.

The Butcher painted a thick wet line of blood across my brow. Marking me. So much blood that it ran stinging into my eyes, fuck I hoped I wasn't about to get hepatitis. My skin crawled all over, wanting to shrink away not from the fluid but from his unwholesome touch. Marked. There wasn't enough bleach in the world for me to ever be clean.

Then my tormentor spun and dashed right through the rear wall of the shed. Wackiest thing I've ever seen; I suppose when you're that massive, the world isn't as stable as it seems to the rest of us. He threw a knee up mid-flight and kicked through the veneer. Ben made a small sound of protest as the rest dropped on our heads.

What the blood-mad Butcher had spotted had been his bride struggling with a tidal wave of blue uniforms as they flooded the yard. Reluctant credit to Pensi, she really pulled out the stops. By the time the scowling Pensi dug Ben and I out the Butcher's wife was standing by the toppled bins, weeping and shock-stunned as officers briefed her on what she'd been sharing her marriage with.

Ben got whisked out front to endure paramedics dabbing at his cheeks and debating stitches. Turned out that was the Butcher's favourite game: to hold a gun and force you to cut off your nose to spite your face. What a colossal dickhole.

Having my eyes irrigated with saline left me feeling artificially refreshed and I hovered like a good spouse. Never mind residual panic left me a bit tetchy, and I think I popped a hernia dashing to the rescue. 'What the hell were you thinking Ben?'

He couldn't meet my eyes which was a pity as they felt so minty bright right now. 'I had to. I had to find out what made *her* ...'

'What? Dead? Because you almost found out.'

'... not *you*.'

This is me. Not ever sick of being the worst. 'Not me. Ok. I get it.'

Sensing trouble with her creepy cop radar Pensi commandeered my elbow and hauled me off to one side, out of conversation-range of the ambulance. You didn't need to step far from civilisation to end up in the dark and cold.

Out here flashlights stabbed back and forth like maddened wasps. Radios squealed at the icy stars as police pursued the Butcher into the night. My forehead itched. I had a bad feeling they might not catch him.

'I want to hear all of it. Now.'

'I didn't think you'd actually bring *all* the police ...'

'How. Did. You. Find. The. Butcher.'

I nodded across the yard at wifey. Pins had loosed hair across her ashen face. 'Older hubby, keeps odd hours. She found another woman's jacket in his shed and hired me — the other me, I mean.'

'So?'

I chuckled sourly. 'Ben figured it out before I did. What my double was that I'd failed to be. Diligent. Kept up with her work. She nailed the Butcher 'cause she was already looking to finger him as a cheating husband.'

'Except it turned out to be a fair bit worse than cheating. Poor woman. Hope you got your fee up front, I have a feeling she won't be paying otherwise.'

I shrugged. 'At least I had the brains to call the cavalry.' No, that wasn't a shrug. Shakes were setting in because my impulsiveness could have got Ben killed. *I should have let the police handle it* warred with *they might not have got there in time*.

'So … they'll be shooting you back where you belong now, right?'

Bile threatened to uproot my teeth and I stared into the dark. Pensi didn't know. No slideshow for her, with her spine humiliatingly chilly in the wind and sixteen point Calibri laying it all out.

'Immigration collapsed my reality. That's how they get the energy to steal someone across.'

'What does that even mean?'

'The reality I belong to is gone.'

Pensi didn't look stricken, because lost universes were too fucking much. More than any normal mind could encompass. And all for the sake of some lost kid, and a family too wealthy to be told no. 'Huh. Like I said, all this science is way past my pay.'

So far as good old meat-and-potatoes and a beer after supper Pensi was concerned she was alive, Ben was alive (even out here we could still hear the swearing), and the souls cramming the houses to either side of us and right down the street, just toodling about their lives. It was only to me that they were all dead. Not only dead, obliterated. Never existed. A horrific abyss where my heart should be.

'So, what now?'

Ah crap. She was serious. Listening to my shadow's husband wincing and moaning in the back of an ambulance.

Somewhere out there was the Brunswick Butcher's fissured face, like a fox in darkness. All ghosts.

I risked a slow breath, that plumed out in frosty curlicues. 'I guess I'll have to make a place for myself right here in hell.'

WHITE PICKET
BP GREGORY

a short story

WHITE PICKET

As the sun slumps, the starving folk in rags love gathering on my lawn. They're waiting for me to drag myself home from work. It's kinda how I've always imagined having a loyal pet might be; only, you know, horrible.

The tall fence throws striped shadows across the road that I feel ought to rattle like speed traps on approach. My Prius spotlights a series of slack faces pressed between the palings and they flinch back into the herd, too roughly, leaving splinters crowning their ears. My welcoming committee. More every day.

All reflect the same misery, like gravity has seized those sad-sack faces for a good yank. And how do they keep slipping by the gate, anyhow? I have to punch in a code and it's my damn house! Leastways a few more decades of cash on the nose, plus interest, will make it so if I don't misstep. Just in time to hop neatly into my grave. And assuming the ever-loving economy doesn't fold first.

Code tendered, the entry gate grudgingly squeals aside. Attracted by the racket the horde abandon their posts, if you'll pardon the pun, and shuffle in my direction. Viewed through the windscreen my driveway quickly becomes a gauntlet of shuddering bones and skin.

Any nearer to an urban hub and my sprawling green lawn would be labelled "squandered" real estate. But in these tender parts a beautiful front yard really says something. You don't go waiting on the council's good graces to see your verge trimmed, either.

The shading hedge hasn't filled in yet, so as I inch forward from the tree-lined street I plunge into the last bit of heat for the day: a bloodied sunlit morass. Hides no detail. Just as the windscreen's aftermarket tint fails to deflect the crowd's eyes burning through to me.

Sweat prickles. I can smell myself in the confines, all mixed up in the upholstery and it's just unbearable. I take a deep quavering breath. The words blown out on it are, 'Here we go.'

FYI revving the engine and mashing the horn does nothing, I've tried both. Nudging them aside with the bumper is the only way to move forward. Hands batter the panelling to all sides of me in eerie silence, with not much more strength than kittens' paws. The only soundtrack being gravel crunching under the tyres, the occasional "POP" of a single rock pinging free to scare me right out of my skin. I must say, the children are the worst, with their little bellies blown up like balloons. Even the threat of a child forces me to avert my watering gaze, lest I witness one slip under.

Stupid driveway! Why are you so long! With such a grand property I'd fantasised a whole new lifestyle: dinner parties with congenial neighbours commiserating on their nine-to-five over spritzers, keeping an indulgent eye on kids of like age romping on the grass with my daughter. Maybe even a dog. I know they're hellishly expensive; pet insurance, and you have to pick up logs; but my lass could do with some responsibility. Get her invested in the care of another living thing.

Instead the lush greenery is entirely lost beneath twisted, blackened feet that wouldn't be out of place on the slopes of Everest. It's sniffing glue that does that, I read somewhere; ruins the circulation but they do it 'cause it make them less hungry. Anyways, we don't dare go out. So what's the point in having a patio?

'Zombi-ies, bees bees bees!' My eight year old sings playfully with her nose to the dining room window. 'Plants'll get 'em: boom! Boom!' My fantasies of her dashing freely through the dusk and having to get called in for dinner were pointless. She's more likely to be upstairs playing some digital game that I don't see the point of.

Nonetheless, I shush her bad manners when it happens. They're not zombies. Just too poor to know better. Of course they are so *many*, and they do kind of look like zombies. They flood. They press against the house. They gasp and wheeze and suck in all the air. The two of us, we camp from room to room and live with the blinds drawn, else they'd stare in all night. It's impossible to eat, to watch a show, to enjoy anything knowing they're out there.

You can just *feel* them. Blinds or no blinds. No good shutting your eyes. A sinking despair comes off them like a miasma, and it mounts without relief as their numbers swell. I kneel all night in the dark with my daughter upstairs like I'm some sort of guard; with them packed so solidly in the yard that their arms can't even stir. Me listening to the house's walls groan in echoes long and deep inside my bones, singing old tales of stress tolerances long exceeded, micro-fractures, the whole nine yards ringed with a nice picket fence. It is like living at the bottom of the ocean. Wondering if it'll be agonising when the bursting point comes, as the whole pressurised house squashes flat.

The garage is achieved, finally. I sit in my Prius numbly contemplating ways to push through their endless ranks to the front door, each more impossible than the last. I'm so knackered from work and from missing sleep that my hands and feet are dead lumps. Almost too much effort to turn the engine off. Fumes are already choking the claustrophobic nook — now there's a way out, I suppose.

All the while the soft insistent *thud thud* against the bodywork. Eyes that I can't meet are waiting on all sides. But it's not like I can call the cops and have them shifted off my grass, or, I don't know … "disposed of," somehow. Because, hey. It's a free country, isn't it.

Look how free they are.

Our Lady of the Trampled Beast

a short horror

BP GREGORY

OUR LADY OF THE TRAMPLED BEAST
ò ó

Four live-long days of tramping scrag brush, getting scratched to hell like I'd tripped into a bushel of cats, and I won't lie. All this hypnotic waving green had somehow along the way switched from being idyllic to downright spooky. Whether it would also be mysterious and ooky remained to be seen. The signs weren't good.

I paused on trembling calves that felt like sticks had been rammed in. Ostensibly tugging my shirt to let sweat dry; actually trying to get my head around another night in this sloppy organic purgatory.

When considered from high-rise safety, this jaunt had seemed a golden opportunity. Just land this one outdoorsy trick, and all those hunched meaty backs between me and the corporate horizon would become leapable.

Given these past ninety-six hours worth of heel blisters spelling *ouch* in bumpy braille, I was now willing to concede I'd been slightly too starved for promotion.

Garry and Jackson, my knights in white satin, chose that stupendously unhelpful moment to start in. 'We're lost, aren't we. Lost! Lost in these fucking trees!'

Nanny-state here rolled my eyes, although they weren't wrong. "Fucking trees" scarcely did these scaly behemoths justice. More like the legs of fossilised dinosaurs looming silently all around us. The trunks had a repulsive muscularity, as though they might uproot at any moment to resume a march aeons in the making.

Even the modest specimens were too broad for my trio to stretch our arms around. We tried, back on day one. When we still had the energy for pissing about. I thought it would make a nice promo shot, the corporate logos on our windbreakers crisp and clear.

We all ended up reeling and brushing frantically to dislodge the pissed-off ants riding shards of diseased bark down our fronts like little surfboards. The photograph managed to perfectly freeze our moment of horrified realisation as the first volcanic stings bit.

Muggins here even received a touch of Good Old Mother Nature right in my mouth the moment I opened wide to swear, because of course I fucking did. A jabbing finger of fuzzy rot that sent bile foaming past my molars. Of scant consolation was that Garry copped the same, as his yap trades twenty-four-seven. 'There's your promo,' he gagged and spat.

Come that evening I lay limp as a rag tangled in my sleeping bag's fetid embrace. My clammy skin knew more than I did, flickering like a mule's rump beset by flies. Paranoia prodded dentition and swore it could still feel some tacky tree residue, in defiance of a whole tube of toothpaste.

I squirmed uncomfortably. Gassy burps. Wood blight scratching at my gut. My wingmen were too delicate to mention exuded odours, but had found excuses to shift their sleeping bags away.

The carry-on continued. 'Cheap-ass PR stunt isn't worth tumbling down some old mineshaft,' moaned the exact same pink-cheeked Garry who, when we'd stood daunted alongside the sedan in our creaking new packs and shoes, had windmilled his arms at the prospect of, and I quote, '... the world's richest deciduous forest!' Nice one, Gary. You utter Wikipedia pillock.

Jackson's woe was transmitted to me solely via inflamed basset hound eyes. In an allergic storm he was humping film equipment strung off every limb, and I'm pretty sure it was killing him. The sensation of Jackson's mournful stare drilling into the back of my neck felt magnitudes worse, somehow, than Garry's wholesome out-and-out bitching.

Groaning back into reluctant motion I tossed my only conceivable response back over my shoulder. 'What is it you gents want outta me, huh?' "Gents" — often in the haze of one foot in front of the other their names genuinely slipped my mind. My stalwart companions devolved into no more than a pair of heavy mouth-breathers crashing in my wake. Sometimes my thighs quavered like they were chasing me. 'This is a stupid PR stunt.'

Climate destruction had inevitably made these *rich deciduous* forests too delicious to leave the scattered locals dug in like ticks any longer. Although that being said, even with the staggering scale of profit on the line trying to picture our office's roll call of stale, male and pale thrashing around out here gave me the hiccupping giggles. Which was where we came strolling in: Garry, Jackson, and me makes three. We snagged the gig not by seniority but by dint of our ability to walk further than your average golf course.

And sticking yours truly out front of our trinity made the kind of sense you can only get on paper. An ornery local *might* hesitate to ventilate a member of the fairer gender come wandering out of the scrub. It wouldn't be the first time I'd relied on charm to dodge a bullet, except, well, not so *literally* bullets before now. I coughed against a woody tickle in my throat.

A big-ass wall. That's what the trees looked like to me. These sheer, densely wooded cliffs like dirty plates stacked up to the clouds were the most eloquent "KEEP OUT" sign on Nature's behalf as I'd ever seen. Not appreciably different to the company's board room, or any of the other barriers I'd found myself crash-dummying into since sprouting tits. If I started respecting walls, hell, I'd never get anything done.

Our ears occasionally hooked the ghosts of high-octane engines, so we at least knew we weren't the last lost souls on earth wandering around out here. When the breeze picked up (making our teeth chatter) the distant screams bounced eerily from peak to peak. Put the wind right up my backside, not to put too fine a point on it.

Garry of course had read a book once, and he got fired up over the class pornography of shine runners. 'Slice a trespasser's nose right off, they will!' Never mind that once we'd plunged into the deep green we never found so much as a fucking road. I chalked the racket up to teens bored out of their provincial minds. Us getting spooked and bolting mindlessly into the gloom wouldn't improve anyone's day.

Garry waved his hand in front of my eyes, interrupting the sour cud of my thoughts. 'Yoo-hoo. Off in fairyland? I *said*, what's that in your teeth?'

'Oh … fuck's sake. Give me a minute.'

I'd squandered all my toothpaste in an orgy of scrubbing following the earlier tree-to-tonsils debacle. Had to deploy a ragged nail instead, dirt-rimed and squeaking at the crevice between incisors. Squeak. Squeeeeak. My nails were long, getting too long. Not that the boys could turn dainty snouts up at my hygiene; not at this range with their gamy aura thickening the downwind breeze.

The brown clot I yanked from my smile glimmered in the palm of my hand. I shuddered, and sucked the evidence back into my mouth before anyone could see.

The great banded owl had been dismembered and rotting in the fallen leaves. Its severed head by its side where it had been flung, still with those intense gold pools for eyes glaring up into the swaying canopy it had been torn from. That fierce gold was how I spotted it.

I had been crouched to pee, making my own gold, half-obscured behind a trunk while B1 and B2 jittered nervously at minimum safe distance. We obsessed over not losing visual contact because, well, that'd be the final straw, wouldn't it? Being alone out here. Might as well lie down and let the fungus have you.

At first I got the mother of all frights. Reflex-peed on my boot in a quick hot squirt, like that was going to save me. And you would too, with your strides down and tender buns hanging in the breeze, to suddenly find big shining feral eyes leering at you.

Then it made for sad realisation, seeing those pieces of a noble and slightly terrifying bird tossed around like garbage. Who knew owls could get so big? This was some kind of goddamn Thunderbird. You could picture it cheerfully swooping off with whole toddlers, no problem.

I've always loved critters. Attributed the welling tears to nostalgia, and not the urine on my foot or generally battered ego. A fraught childhood of righting toppled beetles, and tenderly transporting frogs back to the wet grass verge in my wee fingers. Defiant to the other kids' sniggers. Our Lady of the Trampled Beast.

Audible gut commentary on the state of things grumbled from behind my bellybutton. A quick, guilty peek to ensure Garry and Jackson's backs remained dutifully turned. I yanked up my pants. I had to move fast.

The owl carcass was soft. Aged into the mud. Those bright coins watched sceptically in the dimness as runnels of gore slumped through my scooping fingers.

Urk, my throat protested, *urk*, wanting no part of it. But oh, my stomach did. My stomach was a collapsing star, it wanted the owl so badly.

In my avarice I choked down a few scratchy feathers, making me cough and hack.

'You ok back there?' A thin nervous check-in.

'FINE! Ahem, fine. Nearly done.' I kicked leaves over the owl's head to hide it. *Quit staring at me.*

Innocently dusting off my hands by the time my compadres turned around, relieved to have the amigos together again. Nothing but a single clot in my smile to give me away.

There was no need to trouble the boys with this. Shit, I mean, little wonder I was famished: we'd been walking for days. Walking burned a *ton* of joules, right? Way more than being parked at a desk. No worry whatsoever.

Besides, if one expected to thrive in the office environment shame was a taste to be embraced. Expect it dispensed in acidic foam from the "employee benefits" coffee machine. Feel it linger while enduring an "all in good fun" groping at the after-work mixer, another kind of employee benefit for the higher ups.

Survival required a bipartite brain; sort of like what dolphins did, only less awesome. One part engaged full steam in the here and now ... even if the now consisted of mulch, dead owls and trees, trees, so many trees. Keep the rest of what you've done locked safe in the vault.

ò ó

Garry and Jackson wanted to go back. Great idea, lads. Top points. Oh yes, except that none of us could settle on which way constituted "back." What direction promised to return us safely to our sealed glass tower? I missed its air conditioning, dusty on the tongue you ran over cracked lips as the dehumidifier split you wide open. Vending machines murmuring placidly in the corridors.

Distress boiled off the boys as they swivelled this way and that, sniffling for home. It was like they hadn't even considered I genuinely might not know where I was going. Flattering, I guess.

With the rest of the forest forming a smothering damp moss rag across my senses, my companions' stressful sweat, as of unventilated gym lockers, did something to me. Seemed to invert my face. Awkward flashbacks to tossing through long hormonal nights at fifteen, burning up with visions of boys I scarcely knew.

This regression tempted me to hurl Garry and Jackson to the damp ground and roll in them like some glorious hound. Get that jock strap stench all over. Only I couldn't, could I.

Pink cheeks and basset eyes: these were my colleagues. For better or worse they were relying on me to get shit done.

Dark dreams never hurt anybody. So long as they remained dreamy.

While fatally preoccupied with this nebulous concept of home; and, on a more primal level, for the love of God that *smell*; we took one step, two, still squabbling like strays. Lucky number three dropped all three of us into a bog.

'Actually it's a fen.'

'Shut *up*, Garry.'

Our stiff, chafing boots would never be the same again. They ballooned with glacial sludge that sent petrifying bolts of chill up the legs, like being electrocuted. For a moment you just couldn't breathe. One more step, and the teeming jellied waters might well have swallowed all our problems.

It took linked arms — the first time we'd dared touch one another since the gooey ant tree incident — and some awkward backward shuffling to return our team to dry land. At the water's edge we sat around and sullenly wrung out our socks, wrinkly pudding-like feet exposed to the arctic nip. Cold toes are wonderful for plunging the psyche straight into misery.

I wiped my hand nervously across my mouth. What was in the Wikipedia entry for "trench foot?" I had a sinking feeling it wasn't all kittens and rainbows. Garry would likely know, if I wasn't so scared to pipe up and hear it spoken out loud.

Seeing as we weren't accomplishing much until our footwear dried, we decided to pitch camp for the night. Make the best of a bad situation. Straining gossamer motes past our lips to talk; the bugs must be attracted to the moisture. Squadrons orbited our bowed heads while we worked and sang their neurotic high *eeeee*. All frail wing and no substance. You could gorge on a million, sieve them from the air like some land-going baleen whale, and become only lighter.

By the time the sun slunk away, both lads were settled safe and snoring. All tuckered out. No torches, and the *hnnk* of Jackson's tortured allergies was the camp's only reference point in the dark. The poor boy's head must be a honeycomb of swollen flesh by now. Should rescuers be out searching, they need only follow the cacophony.

If anyone but us was poking around in these fucking trees.

I left my ruined boots and all the rest behind, and waded out into the fen. Groping by touch. I'd never been bold enough to try skinny-dipping while young enough for it to have made any sense. Funny old time of life to be having a mid-crisis. But, as they say, appetite makes fools of us all.

Waist deep would do. I wanted to shuck my duties for a breath, not go off the deep end entirely. I ducked my head — cold! so cold! — to suck brackish water down my searing gullet. A swampy hiss of steam as it hit. Clouds streamed from my nostrils, warm and wet on my face. The bugs loved that.

I closed my eyes and tried to imagine the billions of microscopic lives in each mouthful. Picture them filling me up. Solid, warm belly. Contentment. The power of positive thinking.

Not enough. It would never be enough. I could pour this whole damn fen in with its frogs and midges and never feel any better. My jaw ached from grinding uselessly all day long, teeth craving something in between. My core was a simple funnel leading down into darkness.

Clasping both fists over the insatiable curse of my mouth I rocked there on my heels, with mud and worms squeezed between my toes, in terror of the gaping void. How tiny I found myself all of a sudden. How inadequate. I had always considered my limbs to be sturdy and reliable; now look! They were practically twigs.

I dragged a thick sheaf of my own long dripping hair to my lips to chew. Reflexively tried to swallow. Baffled on a deep fundamental level, because in striding out I had seen exactly how this trip would take me where I wanted to go. I couldn't comprehend how I'd gone so astray.

'Hello? Damn, it's freezing. What are you doing out there?'

Jackson must have overheard my snivelling. Jackson who kept a weather eye out, thinking I was so much like his kid sister. Sure, although I wasn't an attorney or anything. Not nearly so successful as her.

Despite their malingering I liked Jackson and Garry. Even though we hadn't interacted often at work … or ever, really. I wanted them to make it home to their presumed families. Even back to their awful habit of loitering behind my workstation loudly discussing "sport." They'd go on until it was all I could manage not to spin my chair around with a sharp pencil in each fist and bury them between their stupid smug eyes.

My bare back quivered. Jackson was whispering across the midnight pool to me, from the shores of sanity. Worrying with his sad puppy eyes. Calling for me to return. Returning to them was my job: to be lucid, and in charge. To get my team home.

How considerate of him not to wake Garry. The long bones stood out brutally in my arms. Steam around my face. Slick with rank water I turned to show Jackson what I had become.

ò ó

Garry could not get his head around how Jackson had gotten lost in the middle of the night. He glared mistrustfully at the crowding trees as though they were to blame, and honestly, I knew just how he felt.

No, I didn't hear anything either. Perhaps Jackson went for a piss and got turned around? An ordinary, drowsy midnight piss where it would be so easy to lose your way. Definitely no bubbles boiling to the surface of a murky pool, bubbles instead of screams. Pop them and you'd let loose the trapped "aargh!" and "nooo!" sounds from hell. No skin that resisted, wanting to keep the hopes and dreams that made up a human being safe inside. Resisted elastically, then tore, offering up its bounty.

My expression in the face of Garry's panic was bland. No: politely concerned. Not at all the features of someone terrified of what I might shit out later in the day. Fingernails, shards of bone, agony to pass. Pattering along with fresh blood to the bottom of a shameful hole clawed into the waiting earth by my own two hands.

Bury the evidence deep enough, and it might never have happened.

I may as well not have gone to the trouble. Even now, I did not feel satisfied. Hungrier, rather. Beyond the natural revulsion and guilt and humiliation, it was as though the longing and failure of a mid-tier pencil pusher named Jackson had been added to mine, which was plenty already.

I now carried a Jackson-shaped hole. Aching to be filled with everything he had hoped for himself when he glanced in the mirror. A reflection spread thin, like all of us I suppose. Luggage under those eyes you could emigrate with. Never keen to drag himself back to the office but what choice was there?

I carried a hole. And the edges, like damp sand, were crumbling.

The both of us crouched over our little stack of gear, my anxious counsel with Garry consisted of, 'What are we going to do?' stuck on a loop, in increasingly shrill voices. We might have gone on that way until the heat death of the universe were we not interrupted by a thin wavering wail coming from way off in the distance.

Hearing it dried my blood right up. A call lonely and sad and full of scarcely concealed hysteria ... or so my somewhat biased ears interpreted. 'What the actual fuck was that? And just so you know, if you say "moonshine runners" I am going to commit murder.' You know. Again.

'Well, I know my engines ...'

'Sure you do Garry.'

'... and that didn't sound like any kind of car. An animal, maybe?'

'What, like a wolf?'

'Howling at the daytime moon? Haven't been wolves out here for ages.'

'But they're trying to bring them back, right? For biodiversity. All sorts of fucking places.' I belched nervously. Our company's venture would put the kibosh on any such environmental plans, but for obvious reasons I very much wanted Garry to come round to believing Jackson had been dragged off by a wolf. Two wolves, maybe: Jackson was a big dude. A whole avalanche of wolves pouring out of the dark.

Garry didn't seem convinced. 'Sounds bloody starving, whatever it is.'

My face convulsed and I had to turn away, smelling my own meaty breath. It seemed my abject flesh could no longer afford tears. They fell only on the inside and were swallowed up, hot and useless.

My companion was beyond noticing. Too busy scratching mosquito bites into molehills. 'We have to find help, yeah? Report Jackson missing. Get a rescue team out.'

Yes, yes and yes. All reasonable, sane things to do. What actually came out of my mouth was, 'How are we going to lug the fucking camera gear?' My desiccated neural tissue seemed only able to dredge up swears and inanity.

Garry slowly let out all his air like a weary middle-aged tyre, looking the equipment over. A sigh from the pit of his existence. 'As best we can, I suppose. Can't leave it lying around. Docking our pay would put us in hock for years.'

So on we went. Trudging under the extra weight of all of Jackson's crap, and the hopeful assumption that he might eventually turn up. Just be around the next bend, smiling and waving with a cheery, 'What took you two jellybeans so long?'

I wanted that. I longed for it to be true so intensely, it felt like I could split this reality of oversized trees and mountains and grab Jackson by his lapels, yank him through from that parallel universe into ours.

Instead we walked and the trees leaned eagerly over Garry and I. They blotted out the remnants of the sky. Ready to fall down, finally, and crush us struggling ants. Come on. Get it over with.

My knees wobbled. They couldn't *actually* be wider than my thighs, not really. Not given the bare handful of days we'd been at this. I was walking less like a normal person than tipping forward. Lurching toward Garry's industriously bobbing shoulders by thrusting thousand kilo boots forward one after the other.

Reaching with my clawed fingers for his neck. Greasy and red like a slab of raw beef.

Garry half-turned, beaming as though he had sensed me closing in. No, that was my paranoia speaking: he couldn't possibly be tuned in to the welter of my appetite. Not and still bathe me with that redeemer's smile.

'You hear that?'

'What?' I heard nothing past the rasp of void rats gnawing at my innards. Patient sand crumbling like wet sugar around the edge of the hole.

'Barking. Wolves don't bark. Domesticated mutts only.' Garry patted himself down with glee. 'We've found help! Follow me — it's going to be ok.'

Most of the world looked smeary and grey, visual beauty gone from me. 'Ok,' I repeated numbly, stepping in time. Panting. Lightheaded. 'It's going to. Be. Ok.'

A rush, the brush snapping and lashing petulantly. Then the massive jostling trunks fell away to either side and we staggered blinking into the light. It was like we had broken out of a nightmare.

Just look at that sky. All blue, no branches. Azure perfection, floating above a clearing like smooth jade set in the hillside. In place of a gingerbread house we were facing a quaint little — I guess you'd say a log cabin. It seemed a smidge up market to call it a shack. Right where I'd pop one if I were planning my perfect weekend retreat to heaven. Guess it might be a different story when you had to live there year-round without electricity, though.

'It's going to be ok,' I whispered determinedly.

Garry shucked his pack right there at the tree line, with a vigour that was likely to ruin the expensive camera doohickies we'd lugged this far. Abandoning it, he strode forward across the fairy tale grass with the buoyant confidence of white middle management. I had no choice but to stagger along behind.

A black and white collie tied up out front of our rustic destination was barking fit to bust. And the owner was home; a snowy haired old duck just coming out the front door to see what the fuss was about.

The folk of these parts not being silly, I noticed that Nanna-come-lately had an alarmingly lengthy firearm tucked under one wing. But at the sight of us, or more likely me (which had always been the plan), plunging toward her house in our fancy boots she was already leaning the boom stick against the wall to scold her dog.

'Frank! You hush now!'

Two sets of bright worried eyes on our approach. They were unlikely to get many strangers out here; our very presence spelled trouble. Or in Frank's case *smelled* trouble. Grandma kept one gnarled hand on the dog's rope while Frank snarled and lunged. Doubtless he was more reliable than the gun.

In a surprisingly gravelly voice she called out to us, 'Frank here never met any stranger he liked. If you're here to stir problems, I'm of a mind to let him loose.' That would definitely be the end of us. I kind of wanted her to.

Garry skidded to a halt just outside Frank's circle of homicidal canine rage. 'Our … friend … missing,' he gasped. Had to be the furthest he'd run since Taco Bill's two-for-one Fridays on the other side of the city. 'Help?'

Oh, Garry. Who could resist those gormless, pinchable cheeks? Or the hollow-eyed colleague labouring up behind him, like some raggedy subspecies of damsel in distress.

'Let me tie old Frank round back, so's you can come inside.'

Spry for her age — whatever that age even was. In the city you got used to the elderly being sequestered, out of mind and all that. Assured that they were definitely demented and incontinent, the poor dears, and that four grey walls were for the best as they were unable to make out for themselves.

With the way clear Garry hopped up onto the porch like a sprightly cherub. I levered my way painfully on joints that felt ready to rupture and start their new life free of my skin. I glanced underneath into the webby undercroft as I struggled, to find that the cabin stood balanced on four little pillars of stacked stone. It had to be stable; I mean, you wouldn't build that way otherwise; but it sure looked like one good push would send it sprawling into the grass.

Old stones, as old as the hills. Perhaps a cool, mossy stone would stay my belly with its patient weight. Pin me down long enough to rest.

Our hostess held the front door open for us to file in. We obliged gratefully. I ducked my head to avoid eye contact, she had the sharp appraising gaze of an owl.

Garry and I found ourselves in a bright and sunny timber room. I've seen bedsits that were equivalent in living space, although not nearly so kind and welcoming. The area was cleverly divided by curtains and softened by rugs that I'm betting Old Lady Woodcraft here wove herself. No Saturday morning trips to Ikea for her. Or perhaps one of her distant, just as isolated neighbours was to credit. You could picture them coming together once or twice a season when weather permitted to trade what was on hand for what was needed.

Briefly I hallucinated chewing on that woven softness, so vividly that I felt dry fuzz between my teeth. Our hostess was one of those whom my superiors intended to banish into the impoverished landless unknown. Weeping sad tracks through the dust on their cheeks, commemorating every step with the liquid and salt of their bodies.

Their eviction would be no more than cruel history repeating. Allowing it just once had created this world where such things were possible forever. Allow? Hell, plain ordinary folk had jeered the forced First Peoples exodus. The greed lighting up their bellies had let them conveniently forget that some meaner leaner party would always pop up further on down the trail, with a bigger maw, all the better to eat you with my dear. What goes around, comes around, no matter how long it takes.

All unsuspecting, Gramma dipped two mugs into a bucket of water and set them down invitingly on her little table. 'If you don't mind my saying so you two look right done in.' She frowned all the harder when gentleman Garry collapsed into the only chair. He seized first one mug and then the other to down them both with loud snorting and snuffling. 'Can I offer you something t' eat?'

'Oh my, yes,' Garry answered fervently, the greedy sod. 'Yes yes yes.'

At the offer of food my vision broke up, like sun through leaves. By chance I fell back against the door and retained my feet. Had I tripped forward, onto our fairy godmother, I suspect things would have gone very differently. The void within me roared, and I was frail in the face of it.

'Loo?' Was all I could risk, in a strangled voice. My jaw clicked and clacked. Spittle foamed freely down my chin, and in any less extremity I'd have been mortified.

'The outhouse is round back, hon.'

I fled. Leaving took profound effort that felt like tearing off my own arm. Banged the door shut behind me, toppled helplessly from the raised porch and was received by soft meadow grass, like a blessing. If only I were a cow the grass could satisfy me and I'd stay forever.

The gnawing inside wouldn't let me lie still. So, scraping up my sad collection of bones I groped my way timorously around the cabin's outside as though I were a hundred years old, enfeebled. Plop me in a nursing home and let me dribble, doctor. Please. Stuff me with pills. Let me be fed.

Splinters filled my lips, the stinging sensation swimmy and far away. I realised I was chewing desperately at the plank siding as I went. A frenetic energy to my teeth, ticking and tacking. Hoarse barking reached me faintly past the roaring in my ears.

Oh no. Frank.

I slid around the corner, wet as jelly, and there he was. An old dog. I could see that now that I was up close and personal. But he was giving it all he had. His eyes were two rheumy marbles rolling out of a furious blizzard.

Frank had seen some shit in his time, don't you doubt it. And he did not figure on backing down one red inch. He was fixed on dying the same as he had lived for every proud moment: defending his beloved mistress.

My own eyes pricked with tears I could not shed. I suddenly, desperately missed my childhood dog: Teddy the beagle, with the soft velvet ears. Teddy who'd sat tucked under our kitchen table for every meal with eager tail thumping, knowing how love couldn't resist slipping him something. Who had licked tears from my young cheeks as I cried over … what? A skinned knee? A snub? What did I have to cry about?

It's a fact that you can't ever let beagles run off the lead. They're too obsessed with smells, and once they start chasing a good one down they don't have the sense to look up and aren't ever coming back. Teddy was demolished by a car on my ninth birthday. It happened because I was so excited at having guests that I forgot to latch the gate.

Those same party guests, pretty children all in a row dressed up like an adult's idea of dolls, had arrived to find me holding Teddy in the gutter and wailing. The lolly little dollies milled about in confusion, unsurprisingly wanting to be taken home. Needless to say the party was cancelled. My parents received angry phone calls for weeks.

Teddy had whined as I cradled him — not in pain, but with immense frustration that he was unable to reach my tears this time to lick them away. The stretch was impossible with his back broken, and creepers of purple intestine trailing from his hind. Teddy whined, uncomprehending and tragic, and then he died. He was the last dog I ever owned.

Shh I tried to say to angry Frank, *shh* but my mouth was brimming with saliva. I gargled instead. I drowned on myself. The capacity for tenderness had been stripped away, and somewhere a little girl in a stained birthday frock who loved animals was bawling over her broken heart.

Frank's blunt fangs ripped at my arm. It did nothing to dissuade my fingers, hooked like cruel twigs, from snagging hold of his rough coat and pulling him close. Frank shrieked, the most horrible sound I'd heard any living thing make. Every molecule of me that was still me wanted to die.

I had trouble getting through all that fur.

At first.

ò ó

It was a while before thought resurfaced. Guilty, guilty: surely this interlude with Frank had gone on too long for me to reasonably be in the toilet. I had to return before someone came looking.

Step by laboured step I crept my way back around the cabin to the front porch. It wasn't like I wanted to go back inside. What else could I do, though? Perhaps once Garry saw the state of me he could prove himself to be a hidden man of action, and brain me with that nice solid chair he had his backside on. Make an opening for Nanna Backwoods' gun to finish the job, end of saga. I pushed the door open almost eagerly.

And found Garry sat foolishly on the floor inside. So much for the chair. Garry was at the epicentre of a massive explosion of gore.

The stench was incredible. Even to me. Like getting your face stuffed into a butcher shop's discards bin. Flies trailed me in the open door, thrilled to begin their fiesta.

Garry's elderly victim not having been enough, not really, Garry was now starting in with rabid obsession on the tips of his fingers. Hardly a pleasant digestif.

At the hinge's groan he looked up at me, shame faced. Raccoon circles in the cascading slaughterhouse of his face;

he'd rubbed fists in his eyes, like a tired child. 'I think there's something wrong with me.'

'No shit, Garry.' I propped myself against the rough wall, getting out of the way of the fly conga line. Only now was I noticing how drawn my co-worker's formerly jolly features had become. My own must be no better than a thinly varnished skull by now. Oh well. I was hardly going to make Miss Universe, even before we'd walked into the trees.

Garry continued to converse around the hungry squeaking of enamel on knuckle, some real circular breathing shit. The squeal vibrated in my entrails and made me want to scream. 'Here's a crazy thought I want to float past you. Jackson didn't really "go missing." Did he.'

'I guess not.' No benefit in lying now.

'We hung out a bit, but you know, I don't think Jackson even really liked golf.'

An inappropriate guffaw. 'No?'

'Kept getting the terms wrong. I think … I think he just talked golf with me because he knew I took it up to try and make some friends. It hadn't worked out for me. He was a nice guy, yeah? And I hoovered that attention up. Never so much as asked what he was into. Gave nothing back. Guess that's what you get for being kind.'

I winced, remembering their stupid braying laughter in the office, and my own all-consuming anger. I'd even had to lock my pencil sharpener in a drawer. Couldn't resist the temptation to start work on a shiv.

Garry sighed. Examined his stubs, then got industriously back to work, worrying at them. No rest for the wicked. 'This lady only wanted to help us. I even ate her *shoes*. Can you believe that?'

You bet I could. Nodding so hard made me tired, but not any less hungry.

'I'm so alone all the time, you know. At work. At home with the TV on. Hell, even out here. Like there's this vast dried up old borehole inside that I can't plug, not with anything. Anything that's supposed to be nice just makes it tunnel down deeper.'

'Dude, I'm sorry.'

He shrugged. 'I think it was always this way. On the inside. Only difference now is it's on the outside of me now, too, where you can see it. So what I'm gonna do is I'm going to bring my outside in. Put it back the way it's supposed to be. Otherwise I could eat everything, I feel it, honestly. The whole world.'

I barked an exhausted laugh. 'Garry, humanity's already eating the world. Look why we came out here, for fuck's sake.'

'Yeah, but at the very least everyone should get a bite. Not all swallowed up by the greediest.' It was a nice sentiment.

Wearing my murmuring crown of flies, blowing them off my face, I lingered there in the doorway to watch. I wanted to give Garry the bare human dignity of some company during his immolation. Maybe he could tell himself we were friends.

After all, he was doing the right thing. Man of action. I wished I knew what the "right thing" looked like. I wished I knew what could be enough.

If you have ever sat awake and nauseous on a dark night wondering if a mouth can eat itself, let me enlighten you. If it's hungry enough, yeah. If it's hungry. When there's nothing else left.

Once Garry was finished with himself, off I went. Heading back into the trees I'd so recently sworn I never wanted to see again. Too weak to walk, instead hauling myself face-down with fingers dug into the green green grass, paddling with paper straw limbs. My tongue unfurled and dragging so that I could taste every bit of the world passing beneath me.

Before I could return to the office with my desktop and spreadsheets and a lumbering hierarchy I felt I could really get my teeth into now, I had a hundred little appointments to keep in cabins just like this one. Dotted all up and down these mountains. I intended to visit every one of them. Let the directorate try withholding that promotion, then. Let them try keeping me out of the boardroom with barricades made out of chairs and charts and the screaming, oh my, the screaming.

Should some forward-thinking local step onto their porch before then and ventilate me on sight, fairer sex be damned … well. We'd all be very fucking lucky, I guess.

OUR LADY OF THE TRAMPLED BEAST

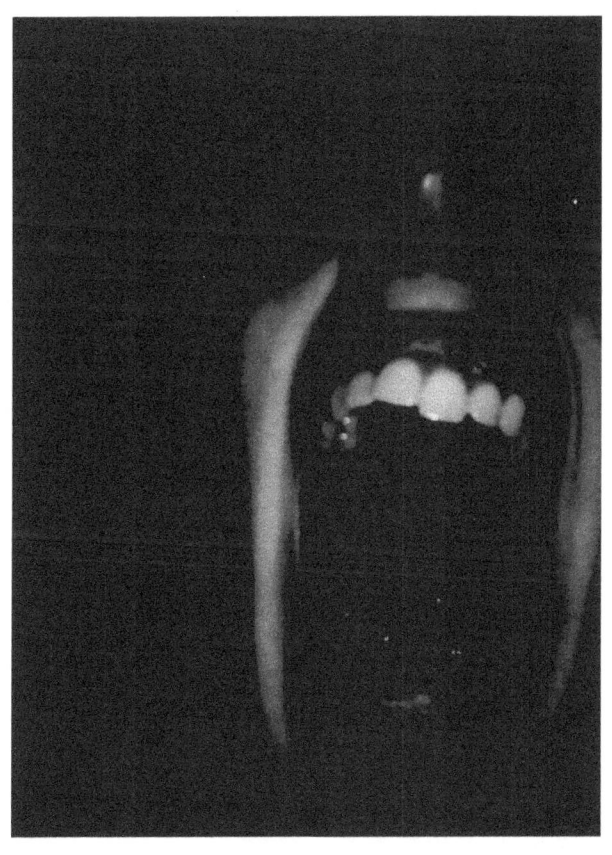

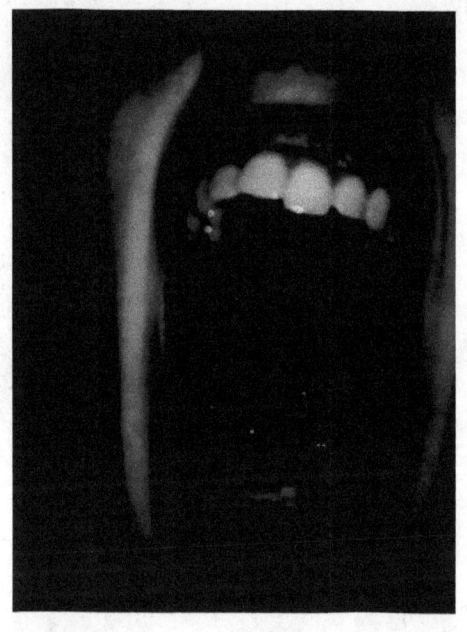

OUR LADY OF THE TRAMPLED BEAST

VU JA DE: COLLECTED SHORT STORIES VOLUME III

OUR LADY OF THE TRAMPLED BEAST

ALSO BY BP GREGORY

New Novel Coming Soon

The Newru Trail

Novels

Flora & Jim
The Town
Something for Everything (Automatons Book #2)
Automatons (Automatons Book #1)
Outermen

Novella

Only Skin

Short Story Collections

Vu Ja De, Collected Short Stories Volume Three
Orotund, Collected Short Stories Volume Two
Cacophony, Collected Short Stories Volume One

The world is frozen
The animals ascendant
And Jim will do anything
to keep his daughter alive

FLORA & jim

BP GREGORY

WHAT MUST A PERSON BECOME to survive the apocalypse?

The world is frozen. The animals ascendant. And, locked in desperate pursuit of "the other father" across a grim icy apocalypse, Jim will do anything to keep his daughter alive.

A PAROLED MONSTER, A PROSTITUTE and a policeman all see a little girl lost, but this isn't the start of a joke. An isolated, frail old man trapped in his apartment; what possible threat could he pose to the sociopaths next door?

Take time for a stroll down humanity's eerie back alleys and enjoy BP Gregory's short science fiction, urban fantasy and horror stories neatly packaged together in Orotund: Collected Short Stories Volume Two.

Author and avid reader BP Gregory brings monsters, machines and roaming cities, insanity, betrayal and lust! With such tales you shouldn't always feel comfortable or safe.

For sneak peeks, more stories, reviews and recommendations as she ploughs through her to-read pile visit bpgregory.com.

www.ingramcontent.com/pod-product-compliance
Lightning Source LLC
LaVergne TN
LVHW012010260326
834688LV00058B/634